RETURN TO SUMMER

Seasons of Summer Novella Series: Book Four

MELISSA BALDWIN

ISBN: 0692931120
ISBN13: 978-0692931127

About Return to Summer

Summertime has arrived, and things are really starting to heat up for me. After a rocky spring, I, Summer Peters, believe I've finally moved on from the heartache of the last year. I adore my new home, my company his thriving, and my relationship with the dashing Alexander Williams is going strong, despite the desperate attempts by others to sabotage it.

But just when I think everything in my life is finally falling into place, I receive another crushing blow, and this time it could affect my business. I know it's finally time to put a stop to the one thing that's threatening my happiness, even if it requires making a very difficult decision. Will this season bring me everything I've always wanted, or will history repeat itself?

Find out how Summer's one-year journey ends in this final installment of the Seasons of Summer Novella

Series from USA Today bestselling author Melissa Baldwin.

I dedicate this book to my little brothers and sisters—Christopher, Adam, Michael, Celestial, Star . . . and to Joseph and Richie in heaven.

Keep your eyes open.

Chapter One

I'm fanning myself with my menu. Summer has arrived, and as much as I love it, I'm never prepared for the brutal heat waves. I open my planner and look through the pages for the next few months. Hopefully me, or rather, my company, Summer Interiors is going to be really busy. It's been quite a year for me, and even as difficult as things have gotten, I wouldn't change anything.

The most exciting thing happening in my life is that after several months of searching, I've found a new apartment. The plan is to move in next month, assuming nothing else gets in the way. Unfortunately, little things seem to keep popping up that make me wonder if this move is a mistake, but I've finally found a place that's the right location and the right price.

The sound of my phone ringing distracts me from my thoughts of moving, and I smile when I see it's my best friend Angie calling.

"I finally get to talk to a real live person," I say sarcastically.

She giggles. "Me, too. I can't believe I haven't even been gone two months yet."

Angie recently moved to Florida. It was unexpected, so we're all still trying to get used to it (me especially). I may or may not have thrown a tantrum, but true best friends are hard to come by. Everyone knows that.

"I know. It feels like an eternity since we've been able to talk."

Angie and I have both been busy, and other than texting, we haven't been able to catch up.

"Well, you're missing a brutal heat wave right now," I tell her while continuing to fan myself. It's so hot that I'm tempted to pour this whole glass of ice water over my head, but I doubt the patrons of this café came here for a wet T-shirt contest. Except maybe the three guys in designer suits who are sitting at the bar. They've been checking out every woman who walks through the door.

She starts to laugh. "Don't talk to me about a heat wave. It's ninety-eight degrees right now, and the only break we will get is when the afternoon thunderstorms roll in."

I have to admit that sounds miserable but I know when winter comes I will be wishing I was there with her.

"What are you up to?" she asks. I close my planner and hold the cold glass of water up to my head.

"I'm waiting on Helena . . . again."

Helena is one of my clients. Summer Interiors has been redecorating her apartment, when I can get in touch with her. She also happens to be my boyfriend's ex-wife, but that's another story. Thankfully, I was able to remove the shrine of their life together from her living room. I admit I used some serious reverse psychology to get her to take it down. Who would have thought she would fall for my lecture on new beginnings and feng shui?

"How's that going?" Angie asks.

"Surprisingly well. She's been much easier to work with than I expected, other than waiting on her like right now."

This is true. I struggled with the decision of working with her, especially after one of her and Alexander's best friends told me they were soul mates and would get back together eventually. We had a few obstacles, but surprisingly she's been one of my easier clients.

"That's good. And how's Alexander?"

I smile to myself. I feel like a giddy teenager when I think about him. We've been together since October, and despite some rocky times, things are good right now.

"He's great."

"And Melanie?"

I sigh. Melanie (Alexander's assistant) would be the one area of our relationship that isn't great.

"She's still here," I say through gritted teeth.

"How can that be? After everything."

I continue to fan myself and take a sip of my water.

"Because she begged him to let her stay. She swore she would never meddle in our lives again and this was the best job she ever had. She laid it on thick, tears and all, and he fell for it. But, I have to admit she's stuck to her word . . . so far anyway."

She groans. "Well, keep your eye on her."

I snort. "Oh trust me, Melanie is not going to make any more trouble for us."

I'm so involved in my conversation that I don't notice Helena has finally arrived.

"Oh, I wouldn't be so sure of that if I were you, love," Helena says, she has a look of dread on her face. "Melanie is diabolical, and you must never let your guard down."

She sits down across from me.

"Hey, Ang, Helena's here. I'll give you a call back later." I quickly hang up, barely giving Angie a chance to say good-bye.

I'm not surprised by Helena's reaction to Melanie; there's certainly no love lost between them.

"I was just talking to my best friend, and she asked me about Melanie. I know there's a lot of bad blood between you."

She folds her arms.

"You don't know the full story, do you?"

I give her a curious look. "About you and Melanie?"

She raises her eyebrows. "I think it's about time for you to hear what really happened with my marriage to Xander. Then, you'll fully understand who Melanie is and who you're dealing with."

My heart sinks at the possibility that there could be more to this whole thing than what I already know. Since the first day I met Alexander and our—ahem—instant attraction to one another began, Melanie has been the constant dark cloud hanging over our relationship.

"Alexander has made things very clear to her. Honestly, I'm not expecting to have any more issues."

Helena orders a bottle of San Pellegrino.

"If only it were that simple," she says, a hint of sarcasm in her voice. "As you know, Xander and I had an amazing marriage."

I furrow my brow. I really hope this isn't going to be another monologue about the perfect marriage of Alexander and Helena Williams. I can't even count how many times I've heard about how passionate and intense their connection was. They never came out and told me the details about their sex life, but I can read between the lines. The story is they grew apart as the intensity began to fade. In addition to that, Melanie's constant presence put a strain on their marriage. And after almost a year with Alexander, I totally understand how that could happen.

"Mmmhmm," I say, while trying not to make eye contact. I'm silently praying this conversation isn't going to get awkward.

"I can't even count the number of times Xander would talk to her over and over again and things would get better . . . for a time."

This is nothing new. I've heard this before.

"Melanie would create different situations or a crisis that would require Alexander's immediate attention. That was her way of dragging him away, and it usually worked. It didn't help that he was trying to grow his business at the time. This made everything urgent and Melanie knew that."

I listen intently as Helena relives the events that lead to her marriage falling apart.

"Then, there were the photographs."

Photographs? What's she talking about?

"What photos?" I ask, suddenly feeling nauseous. Helena came to the States from Sweden to model, but I don't think she's referring to photos from her modeling days.

She gets a pained look on her face.

"One day, I had lunch with a friend from university. It was completely innocent," she trails off. "Not long after our meeting, some photos surfaced of my friend and me in what appeared to be an intimate encounter. To this day, I believe she was behind those photos. She wanted to destroy my reputation and my marriage."

"Wait. You think she took them?"

She sips her Pellegrino and nods her head. "I'm not sure she took them herself, but I believe she was behind the whole thing. It was obvious they were doctored, and even Alexander could see that."

I'm completely speechless.

"Anyhow, I accused her, which made Xander very upset with me. Let's just say she accomplished exactly what she wanted."

Wow. Okay, so I knew Melanie was a jealous, but I never thought she would stoop as low as fabricating photos to sabotage Alexander's marriage. Maybe I should ask Helena about Melanie's relationship with Alexander's mom. I haven't even touched on this subject. That was another whole issue that happened a few months ago when Melanie rejoiced in getting under my skin by pretending to besties with his mom. I'm not proud to admit we almost had a brawl at Pottery Barn, not one of my finest moments.

"My point is you should not let your guard down when it comes to Melanie. Even if Alexander has assured you that he has it under control." Helena says, dragging me out of my thoughts.

I nod my head slowly.

Before I know it, Helena has moved on to talking about her apartment and abandoned all talk about Melanie. Of course, I'm still thinking about it. The problem is there is nothing I can do about it except wait and see what happens. I can't believe I have to sit here and wait for the possibility of someone sabotaging my relationship.

"Oh, and we have to change the rugs in the guest bathroom," she demands, as if her life depended on it. "That spoiled, self-absorbed Valynn has the same ones. The last thing I want is for her to think I copied her."

I zone out while Helena continues rambling about her *friend* Valynn and her bathroom rug.

Why do I feel like I'm waiting for the inevitable when it comes to Melanie? One thing is for sure, Helena may have let her succeed in destroying her relationship but I won't. I will do whatever it takes to make sure she doesn't come between Alexander and me.

Chapter Two

I don't know what I was thinking? I look around at the sea of boxes, newspaper, and junk I've somehow accumulated over the years. I have no idea how or when I got this stuff? And do I really need nine flower vases? Probably not.

It's actually been somewhat of an emotional experience packing up my apartment. Especially when I come across a box of things from my eighteen months with Jake. I even saved the napkin from our first date. (Lame, I know.) If I had a backyard, I would totally do a bonfire. I continue to sort through the random items in the box—a small stuffed animal he won at a carnival, some clothes, and an envelope at the bottom of the box.

I sit down, leaning up against the wall. I hold the envelope in my hands like it's an important document. I contemplate opening it or just throwing it away.

Unfortunately, my curiosity gets the best of me. When I finally open it, I remember exactly why I saved it. It's a card from our sixth-month anniversary, and Jake wrote the sweetest note about how much richer his life was having me in it. Reading this, I would have never suspected that a year later he would blindside me by dumping me while on a vacation. A few months ago, this note would have brought me to tears, but not anymore. This is probably because I'm finally feeling more secure with Alexander. It's been difficult to not be paranoid in my new relationship after what happened with Jake. And of course, Melanie's involvement doesn't help.

I take a deep breath and slowly tear the card in half. Who would have thought it would feel this amazing to throw something away? I feel as if I just climbed to the top of Mount Everest. I'm about to text Angie, and then catch myself. I know I can still text her, but it's not like we can meet up at the coffee shop to celebrate my huge breakthrough. Alexander is in LA for work this week, and suddenly I feel very lonely. I want to share my news with someone. Hmm . . . there is someone I can tell, but I'm not sure I want to open that can of worms tonight. After much thought, I abandon my packing and make my way downstairs. I can hear the sound of ocean waves crashing through the door, so I knock loudly. The music stops, and a few seconds later my landlord, Mrs. Rothera, opens the door.

"Hiya," she says warmly. She gives me a questioning look, and I'm pretty sure she's watching my aura or body language to figure out the reason for my unexpected visit. I try not to make too many visits to her because it's usually somewhat of an ordeal. As nice as Mrs. Rothera is, she tends to stick her nose into my personal life and offer up a dose of unsolicited advice. Although, I guess that's what psychics do.

Yep, she's a psychic. She's legit, too; at least, that's what I've heard from all my friends who have had readings from her. I haven't actually had a reading because the thought of knowing stuff about my future makes me nervous. She's given me hints here and there but that's as far as I've let it go.

"Am I bothering you?"

She shakes her head and pulls me through the door.

"You know you're always welcome here." She pauses. "Hopefully, you've come to tell me that you've changed your mind about moving out?"

I laugh nervously. "Not exactly. Actually, I was looking through some boxes tonight and I found something . . . a note from Jake."

She raises her eyebrows.

"And?"

"And, it didn't bother me. In fact, I threw it away. For the first time in almost a year I feel like I've finally moved on from my heartbreak. I think I've finally turned a corner."

She nods slowly, and I know her well enough to know she has something to say.

"Good for you. How does it feel?"

I smile. "It feels amazing. It almost feels like it was exactly what I needed to close this chapter of my life."

I know I'm being really dramatic over throwing away an old card, but doing this reminds me of how far I've come.

Mrs. Rothera closes her eyes and sits very still. I really hate it when she does this. One of these days I'm afraid she's going to open her eyes and claim she's someone else, as in someone else will take over her body. For some reason, I always think about that scene in the movie *Ghost* where the spirit jumps into the psychic's body to talk to his wife.

I'm relieved when Mrs. Rothera opens her eyes and she's still herself.

"Anyway, I'm proud of you." She quickly stands up and walks toward the door. "I hate to do this but I have to get to my meditation and turn in early tonight."

Wait. What the hell just happened?

"Oh, okay." I reluctantly stand up.

"Thanks for listening."

She gives me a half smile. "Of course. Keep me posted on the moving plans."

I barely have a chance to say good night before she shuts the door in my face. I'm so confused right now. I don't think Mrs. Rothera has ever rushed me out like that before. She must really be upset about me moving, but I can't let that distract me from my plans. If throwing away the letter proves anything, it's that I know I'm ready to move forward with my life and I couldn't be happier about it.

"One more day, baby. I can't wait to wrap my arms around you."

I'm sitting in the office I share with my friend Gina, and I'm trying to tone down my giddiness. I absolutely love talking to Alexander on the phone. He has the sexiest voice, and of course when he says things like this, it totally makes my heart race.

"One day is too long," I whine.

I glance over my shoulder to see Gina making gagging motions. Like she has room to talk. She hooked up with Angie's cousin Vinny at the good-bye party I threw for Angie and Brett. I know for a fact they are very open with their PDA—kissing, wandering hands, and who knows what else has gone down in public places.

"Are you still planning to meet me at the house?" he asks.

"I sure am. I have a meeting with a client, but I plan to head over there right after."

"Good because I will be ready to spend the whole evening with you."

When we get off the phone, my face hurts from smiling so much.

"You two are so adorable. It's almost nauseating," Gina says playfully.

I roll my eyes. "Don't even start in on me. You and Vinny are lucky you haven't been arrested for public indecency."

She shrugs her shoulders. Typical Gina, I know she wouldn't care if she were arrested. Although, I'm sure she never would be. Her family is well connected with the law enforcement in our small Connecticut town, not to mention even more connected in New York City. Whether that's good or bad I'm not clear, and I don't ask.

"Speaking of nauseating, I have to tell you about what I found last night. You're going to be so proud of me."

I tell her all about finding the box of Jake's things and ripping up the note. She gives me a high five, but she definitely isn't as excited as I am about it. I guess it's hard for other people to understand exactly how big of a deal this is for me.

"So, you finally realize that Jake did you a favor by showing you what an ass he is."

I giggle. "I guess so. I was so excited I needed to tell someone, so I went downstairs to tell Mrs. Rothera."

She gives me a funny look. "Really?"

"I know, right? Anyway, at first she was really nice. Invited me in like she usually does, and then she got weird."

"What do you mean weird? Weirder than she usually is?"

I love Gina's honestly. No matter how brutal it is, I can always count on her to give it to me straight.

"I can't explain it. One minute we were just talking, then she closed her eyes, and then she rushed me out."

As I tell her what happened, it makes me even more confused. Maybe she had some kind of vision or weird psychic moment. She knows I don't like to hear things about my future so maybe she wanted to get rid of me before she blurted something out.

"Are you going to ask her what happened?" Gina asks, barely looking up from her phone. It's obvious she's losing interest in our conversation.

"We'll see. She's probably still mad that I'm moving out."

After how strange she was acting last night, I really hope that's all it is.

Chapter Three

I really enjoy my job, but sometimes I end up with the most difficult clients, and unfortunately you never know until you start working with them. I know this comes with the territory and not everyone is going to be flexible and easy. My newest client, Valerie, is definitely difficult. She contacted me about a month ago and insisted that she had picked Summer Interiors over *several* other interior decorators. According to her, my company has been the talk of the town and she knew she *had* to work with me because she only works with the best. I appreciate her stroking my ego but that should have been a red flag for me.

Don't get me wrong, she was very nice, but the moment I set foot in her home, she became super high maintenance.

The biggest issue we're having is that she picks out the most expensive décor, and then complains about the cost of everything. Not to mention she calls or texts me several times a day with random, unimportant questions. A few occasions have been so irritating I've considered telling her I can't work with her anymore. The problem is she's already recommended me to quite a few of her friends. I continue to remind myself that if I can work with Alexander's ex-wife, I can certainly work with Valerie and her unreasonable requests. After a particular frustrating day searching for the exact mirror she wants for her formal living room, I'm more than ready to see Alexander later tonight.

"This one is close, but it's still not the exact frame I'm looking for," Valerie whines. I contemplate throwing the laptop against the wall but refrain from expressing my frustration in such a childish manner.

"We will find it, don't worry," I say, trying to reassure her.

I zone out as she continues scrolling through pictures on her quest to find this perfect, one-of-a-kind mirror. My thoughts bounce back and forth between my move and Mrs. Rothera's odd behavior from the other night. I'm still so confused about why she flipped the switch so quickly. Maybe I should take Gina's advice and ask her about it.

"Wait. This is it," Valerie shouts, snapping me out of my thoughts.

I'm about to jump up and cheer, but I stop myself. I've already been short with her today, and I need to maintain my stellar reputation. (Her description, not mine.)

"Awesome," I say, glancing at the mirror. Honestly, it looks exactly like the thirty other mirrors we've looked at.

"It's perfect, don't you think?"

I purse my lips. "Absolutely."

She's about to say something when she gets a text message. She glances at her phone and a strange expression comes across her face.

"I have to make a quick phone call. I'll be right back."

She rushes off to the kitchen, so I start to gather up my things. I glance at the time and my pulse picks up, only a few more hours until Alexander arrives home. I reach for my bag and accidently knock over my glass of water. Crap!

I quickly move my laptop out of the path of the flood and rush to the kitchen to get a towel. I stop in my tracks when I overhear Valerie on the phone.

"Don't worry, Mel. I got this," she whispers. "Yes. You know you can count on me."

Mel? For some reason Melanie pops into my head. Could she be talking to Melanie—as in my arch nemesis? Maybe I'm just being paranoid, but it wouldn't be surprising if she knew Melanie. She told me she was referred through a friend of a friend.

I hear her say good-bye, so I count to three and hurry into the kitchen.

"Hey, Valerie," I call. "Can I have a towel? I'm so clumsy. I just spilled my water."

Her eyes grow wide as if she was just caught her robbing a bank. She had to be talking to Melanie, otherwise she wouldn't look so guilty.

"Oh . . . um . . . sure," she says nervously. She hands me a few towels, and then follows me back to the dining room to help me clean up the mess.

I leave about fifteen minutes later without any explanation for the secret phone call. Whoever Valerie was talking to, she obviously didn't want me to hear.

I spend my entire ride home (to Alexander's home) giving myself a pep talk. I refuse to let this worry me, and I certainly refuse to let it affect my evening with Alexander. Melanie has ruined one too many nights we've had together and from now on that's going to change.

After making myself a cup of tea, I curl up on Alexander's couch with my laptop while I wait semi-patiently for him to get home from his trip. Of course, his flight is delayed, so I have several hours to kill before he's home. I decide to use this time to search some ideas for decorating my new apartment. I find it funny that I have no issues decorating other people's homes, but when it comes to my own home, I stare at a blank page.

I lose interest pretty quickly and start to think about Valerie whispering on the phone today. I decide to look up Valerie's online profile and pictures. I know I'm totally trolling, but if Helena is right, then I need to keep an eye on Melanie and that would include her friends. Sure enough, Melanie is listed on Valerie's contact list. I know that doesn't guarantee that she was talking to her on the phone today, but she was definitely whispering for some reason, not to mention she left the room rather abruptly.

I must doze off because the next thing I know someone is touching my face. When I open my eyes, I see Alexander sitting on the edge of the couch leaning over me.

I practically jump up and wrap my arms around his neck.

"Mmmm . . . this is exactly what I've been waiting for," he says into my neck.

When I finally loosen my grip and pull away, he takes my face in his hands and kisses me gently.

"I'm sorry it's so late," he says, rubbing his eyes. "Today was one of the longest travel days I've ever had. And I was extra impatient to see you, so that made the day even longer." He sits down, pulling my legs onto his lap, and leans his head on the back of the couch.

I start to run my hand through his hair. One thing's for sure, I will never get tired of looking at him. With his dark hair and blue eyes, he could be Superman's twin.

"Why don't you go to sleep? We can talk tomorrow," I tell him.

He shakes his head, but I can see the exhaustion. He's trying to stay awake for me.

"It's okay," I tell him. "You can barely keep your eyes open."

"Okay, but on one condition," he mumbles.

I smile. "Condition? What condition is that?"

"You stay with me tonight," he begs. "Please."

I smile. "There's no place I'd rather be."

As I lie still, listening to Alexander's gentle snoring, I can't help but feel incredibly happy. Being in love will do that to you, and I guess I never thought I could feel this way again after what Jake did. Boy was I wrong.

Tonight didn't go the way I had hoped, being that I spent maybe twenty minutes with Alexander before he crashed, but I still feel grateful. This is exactly the point I've been waiting to get to because no matter what Melanie tries to pull, I'm more than ready for my future, a future with Alexander.

I wish I could stay here all day. It's a beautiful morning, and I'm sitting on Alexander's patio planning out my day. The only thing that would make it more perfect would be to spend it *with* Alexander. Unfortunately, he's been on the phone most of the morning. I know it's his first day back in town after a week so I can't expect him to spend the entire day lounging around with me, although that would be awesome.

"I'm sorry," Alexander says, interrupting my thoughts. "I'm supposed to be out here having breakfast with you."

I force a smile. This isn't the exact homecoming I was hoping for, but I'm certainly not going to make him feel bad about it.

"It's okay."

He shakes his head. "No, it's not. I can at least take a break during breakfast. I told Melanie to hold calls until later."

A few months ago, she would've been calling him every two minutes, but since Alexander had his long talk with her, she's been more respectful of his personal life. This gives me hope that Helena is wrong and we've turned a corner once and for all.

"What are your plans for the day?" he asks, taking a sip of his coffee.

"Well, I have to try to get some packing done, and I have a few things to do for my new client."

"Oh yeah. Which new client is this?"

I groan. "Her name is Valerie Watson. I totally regret taking her on as a client. It's been a month and we haven't made any progress. We just keep going around in circles."

He makes a face. "Mmmhmm . . . I know Valerie, and yes, she can be a lot to take."

I give him a curious look. "How do you know her?"

He gives me a thoughtful look.

"You know I don't even remember where I met her, probably some social event. She's one of Melanie's good friends."

A-ha. I knew Valerie was talking to Melanie yesterday. That would make sense as to why she looked so guilty when I walked into the kitchen. Valerie and Melanie are besties, how cute. Ugh.

"Summer?"

Alexander interrupts my thoughts.

"Sorry. I was . . ."

I just can't tell him about my theory. I promised I would trust him and let him handle Melanie. But this makes me wonder why Valerie hired me and whether is Melanie involved?

Alexander looks skeptical. "You got awfully quiet all of a sudden. You might as well tell me what's going on in that brain of yours."

I laugh nervously. "It's not a big deal. I just overheard Valerie on the phone yesterday. She was whispering and . . . well, I think she was talking to Melanie."

"And?"

I shrug my shoulders. He looks totally confused.

"What did you hear?"

Crap. I knew I would regret this. I promised him I wouldn't let it get to me anymore.

"She said, 'you count on me' and that she 'would take care of it.'" I pause. "I don't know what she was talking about, but she was whispering, and she had the look of sheer panic on her face when I walked in."

Alexander is quiet, which makes me nervous. He's either thinking about Valerie's conversation or he's thinking that I've completely lost my mind. Or maybe both?

He reaches over and takes my hand. "Baby, I promised you that Melanie wouldn't be interfering in our relationship anymore. I made myself very clear to her, so I don't think she would dare try anything."

I nod slowly. "I know, and things have been better. I just had a weird feeling yesterday."

He pulls my hand up to his lips and kisses it. "I love you, and I'm committed to you. Nothing is going to get in the way of that." I give him a grateful smile.

"So, give me an update on the moving plans. How has Mrs. Rothera been?"

Wow. He changed the subject fast.

The mention of Mrs. Rothera totally reminds me of her strange behavior while I was at her apartment.

"Interesting you should ask. I thought she was doing okay until the other night."

I explain how she abruptly rushed me out of her apartment.

"She loves having you there. Which I can totally understand, if you were living with me I would never want you to leave."

I start to choke on my orange juice. This is the first time there has been any mention of me living with Alexander except for when Angie was convinced he was going to ask me to move in. Obviously that never happened.

"Are you okay?" he asks, patting me on the back.

"Um . . . yeah," I say, clearing my throat.

"She will have to get used to the idea because moving day will be here before we know it."

Before Alexander can say anything else, his phone starts ringing. I guess that's a sign that our intimate breakfast is over.

I begin to zone out again while Alexander takes his call. The truth is I don't want to read too much into what Alexander said. He was probably speaking hypothetically because we've never discussed me moving in and he's never asked. And it's not like I would want to rush anything. Things are good the way they are right now.

Chapter Four

"I told you," Angie says loudly. I have to pull the phone away from my ear. I swear sometimes she's so loud I feel like I could hear her from thousands of miles away, without the phone.

"Why don't you just bring it up to him? You know you want to."

I just finished telling her what Alexander said about me living with him, and I'm definitely not surprised by her reaction.

"I'm not going to bring it up. I don't think he meant anything by it. It was totally hypothetical," I say cautiously.

"What if it wasn't? What if he was giving you that hint to feel you out?"

I stretch out on my bed and throw my arm over my eyes.

"And how many times have you told me that he never liked any of the apartments you picked out? Weren't they all too far away or too small or too old?"

I cringe. I did mention his constant disapproval of the apartments I've looked at, and Angie practically has a photographic memory. She can probably remember what she was wearing the second day of high school.

"Yes, he did, but that was mostly me. It took me forever to find a place I liked. And for your information, he doesn't have an issue with the apartment I finally decided on, so your theory really doesn't hold up." Of course, he hasn't seen my new apartment yet, but I don't tell her that.

"On another note, I have a feeling Melanie is up to her old tricks. And she's bringing in reinforcements again."

This is a good way to change the subject from the topic of me moving in with Alexander.

"What did she do this time?" I can tell by the tone in her voice that she's not surprised and she's quickly becoming disinterested in the never-ending saga of Melanie. Not that I blame her, because I'm over it, too.

"I'm not exactly sure, but I have a weird feeling about my new client."

I tell her about walking in on Valerie's conversation and about her being friends with Melanie.

"Summer, this is ridiculous," she shouts. "Alexander needs to get rid of her once and for all. How long are you going to put up with it?"

I don't say anything. This is not the first conversation we've had about this, and I can't say I disagree with her.

"He talked to her already and things have been better." I trail off. "And I don't know for sure that Valerie and she are up to anything. It was just strange."

"Come on. You know better than that, you wouldn't have this feeling if it were nothing. Remember what happened with Jake? She even pretended to be in a relationship with your ex. It doesn't get much more twisted than that."

"Well, what should I do then?"

I don't know why I'm asking Angie what I should do. She'll probably tell me to hire a private investigator or something completely over-the-top like that.

"Well, first you need to find out if there's something to all of this, and then when you have the proof that this Valerie is up to something, you need to give Alexander an ultimatum."

An ultimatum? As in Melanie goes once and for all?

"You know I can't make him choose. We've already been through this."

"That's crazy. You absolutely can ask him to choose. How long are you going to let her be a hindrance in your relationship?"

I groan.

"Summer, I have to go. Just think about it, okay?"

As soon as I hang up, I realize that familiar feeling of uncertainty has crept up again. I know Angie is looking out for me, but she may be taking things overboard. I'm not saying that I haven't thought about it. There have been several instances when I've almost told Alexander that Melanie needs to go or I go. I just don't want to jump to a conclusion without any proof. And things have been better lately; she's definitely been keeping her distance. For now, I need to live up to this fantastic reputation that Valerie keeps referring to, and hopefully I will find out if there is anything to that phone call.

I look around my living room and I have to admit I'm proud of myself. In the corner are four neatly packed boxes. I've wrapped the fragile items and purged quite a few things. Everyday I get a little closer to my move. And speaking of my move, it's been days since I've seen Mrs. Rothera. I'm sure she's been trying to ignore all the noise of me moving things around, one of the joys of living in a downstairs apartment. I probably should check in on her, especially after our last interaction. As frustrating as she can be, I'm going to miss her. I hop off the couch and make my way downstairs. For some reason, tonight it feels like I'm walking into a storm. I don't hear any weird music or the sound of tambourines coming from her apartment, but I still knock loudly on the door. She could be in some deep meditation, so I wait patiently. A few minutes go by and she doesn't answer. Maybe she's out? I head back upstairs, but for some reason I can't shake this strange feeling. Mrs. Rothera is clearly avoiding me, and I want to know why.

When I get back to my apartment, I don't return to my packing. I pick up my phone and try calling Mrs. Rothera. The call goes straight to voicemail, so I leave her a short message letting her know I stopped by and want to chat with her.

I stretch out on the couch and send a text to Alexander. He said he would be in and out of meetings all day but hopefully he's finished by now.

Not even two minutes go by when my phone rings. I smile to myself.

"Hey, babe. I was just thinking about you."

"Oh really?" I reply flirtatiously.

"Yes, I was thinking about taking you to dinner to make up for our interrupted breakfast."

I look around my apartment, and I know I should continue packing, but an evening out with Alexander is so much more enticing."

"I would love it."

I quickly get off the phone so I can get ready. I don't mention Mrs. Rothera to Alexander yet. I can't stress myself over nothing, and if she is upset about me moving I can't control that. I've been planning this for a while and I'm confident this is the right step for my future.

~

"Babe, you look perfect," Alexander says, wrapping me up in his arms. Now that he's here I'm even more excited for a night out with him. No jetlag, no work, and no Melanie.

He looks around my apartment.

"Wow, look at this place. It's starting to look empty."

I nod. "Yep. I will be out of here before I know it."

He sits down on the couch and stretches his arms out. "So, when do I get to see your new place?"

I smile as I sit down on the edge of the couch.

"We could check it out after dinner?"

"Let's do it."

On our way out the door, we run into Mrs. Rothera. I'm not sure why, but she looks surprised to see me or maybe she's disappointed? How long did she think she was going to avoid me? I do live in her building, right downstairs from her. The crazy thing is that a few short weeks ago I couldn't get away from her.

"Hi, Mrs. Rothera, I just left you a message."

"I'm sorry. I haven't checked my messages yet," she replies coldly.

I wave my hand. "It's fine. I just wanted to make sure you're okay. It seems like we keep missing each other."

She awkwardly checks her mailbox, which is empty. I would stake my life on it that she already picked up her mail hours ago.

"I'm doing just fine. I've been caught up in my work."

I glance at Alexander who's stayed quiet. He raises his eyebrows at me.

"We probably should get going," he says, pointedly. "Good night, Mrs. Rothera."

She smiles warmly at him. "Have a nice evening."

Once we're safely in the car, I ask Alexander if he thinks Mrs. Rothera was acting strange.

"She definitely didn't seem like herself."

That at least makes me feel better knowing I'm not imagining her odd behavior.

"It's weird, isn't it? She's normally so much more engaging. The Mrs. Rothera I know would be asking us every detail about our night."

Alexander makes a face.

"Well, she knows how you feel about all the psychic stuff, so maybe she's respecting that?"

I chew on my bottom lip.

"Maybe, but why now all of a sudden?" I pause. "No, there's more to it. I think she's been avoiding me on purpose."

Alexander casually changes the subject. I know he doesn't want to spend another evening talking about my landlord and neither do I.

After a wonderful and *uninterrupted* dinner, I give Alexander directions to my new apartment. I'm so excited for him to see it I can barely sit still. This will prove to Angie that he doesn't have an issue with every apartment I choose. And why is it a big deal anyway? We don't need to live together to prove we're committed to each other.

"Turn here and the complex is on the right. Isn't this area gorgeous? All fresh and new?"

Alexander laughs nervously. I'm not sure what's so funny.

"It's a great place, Sum."

I give him a curious look.

"Why are you laughing?"

"Don't freak out okay."

Crap. Everyone knows when someone tells you not to freak out the first thing you do is freak out.

"What?"

"Melanie lives here."

Shit.

I put my face in my hands and shake my head. Okay, before I curl up into the fetal position, this really isn't a big deal. So she lives here in this complex. It's a big place, and what are the chances I will see her? Probably never.

"That's fine," I reply nonchalantly. "Um, do you know which building she's in?"

He gives me a side-glance.

"Which building are you in?"

I punch him on the arm. "Very funny. I'm in building eight, apartment one zero one. I finally have a downstairs apartment."

Alexander covers his mouth with his hand. Oh, please no.

"Don't even joke about that," I shout. He hasn't said anything yet, but I know he's probably going to make some joke about Melanie living next door to me.

"Melanie lives in building eight, apartment two zero three"

"Haha. Okay, you've had your fun." I roll my eyes.

But then I notice that he's not laughing anymore.

And there it is. All my joy is sucked out in a matter of seconds. Alexander must notice that I'm practically on the verge of tears. I know I shouldn't let it bother me, but seriously? Will I ever be free of this woman? Is she going to be a permanent fixture in my life? What about when Alexander comes over? Is she going to stop by all the time? Suddenly, Angie's ultimatum idea isn't looking so bad.

"Babe, don't let it get you down. I'm sure you'll never see each other."

This is crazy. Alexander may not have a problem with this apartment, but I certainly do. I would prefer to be as far away from Melanie as possible.

I shrug my shoulders. "I guess. Maybe I can switch apartments. I will call the leasing office first thing in the morning."

This really sucks because I really liked the location of my apartment. It's right on the edge of the complex. next to the woods with a beautiful view.

"Come on. I don't think you need to do that," he insists.

Am I being completely ridiculous? Maybe I am.

"I'll think about it."

He parks the car in front of building eight, and I stare at the building where Melanie and I will be neighbors. Ugh, that sounds completely miserable.

Alexander reaches for my hand.

"I'm sorry. This is all my fault."

I can't disagree with him. Unfortunately, his unorthodox working relationship with Melanie has led us to this point. I stare out the window and think about this new obstacle (at least, an obstacle in my mind) in the way of my move.

"I'm being ridiculous, I know."

He leans his head back against the seat. "It's okay. But I have an idea how to solve all of this."

I give him a curious look.

"What's your idea?"

All of a sudden, my phone starts to ring. Talk about bad timing.

I search for my phone in my bag, and as soon as I see it's a call from Mrs. Rothera I have a feeling I should answer it.

"Hello."

"Hello, Summer. I'm sorry to bother you on your date. I just wanted to let you know I received your message, and I was hoping we could sit down and chat tomorrow. I would like to settle the details of your move."

I look out the window at my new home, and suddenly I'm filled with doubt.

"Um . . . okay. I have a meeting with a client in the morning, but I will be available later in the afternoon."

Hopefully by then I will be feeling better about my decision. I'm starting to sweat. It could be the humidity or it could be my nerves. Either way this is really happening, so I better be sure about my decision.

"I'm sorry," I apologize to Alexander. "Believe it or not, it sounds like Mrs. Rothera is ready for me to leave. We're meeting tomorrow to discuss everything."

I sigh loudly. "I need a vacation."

"Let's do it," he exclaims.

I stare at him blankly. Is he asking me to go on vacation with him? Not that I wouldn't love to go somewhere with him alone—away from Melanie, Helena, Jake, and Mrs. Rothera. The one thing holding me back is the last summer vacation I took with a man; it didn't turn out so great.

"Are you serious?"

He throws his head back in laughter.

"Of course I'm serious. Where would you like to go?"

"Hah. Where don't I want to go?" The past few summers we've gone to Angie's aunt's beach house, but this year we have no plans since Angie's moved. "I don't know, anywhere alone with you would be amazing."

He gives a thoughtful look. "Okay, you pick the location and we'll book it."

I'm so excited I can hardly stand it. I love summertime, and I can't wait to enjoy our first vacation together. The rest of the evening we discuss our vacation, and this is the perfect distraction to keep me from stressing about Melanie being my neighbor.

Chapter Five

*T*his really sucks. As soon as my fantastic evening ends I start worrying again. It feels like that's all I've been doing since last summer. Constantly looking over my shoulder—waiting for something to interfere with my happiness.

How am I going to live in the same building as Melanie? I wouldn't put it past her to use this to her advantage, another tool to worm her way into my personal life. She's already proven that she will take whatever drastic measures she needs in order to keep herself in Alexander's life.

As soon as I wake up, I make myself a cup of coffee and place a call to the leasing office at the complex. I practically beg them to let me rent a different apartment. If I were there in person, I would probably be on my knees begging. Unfortunately, they don't have any other apartments available for another six months, and they offer to add me to a waiting list. I strongly consider resorting to tears and bribes but I refrain. I don't have long to worry because I have to get ready for my appointment with Valerie. For the first time since I took this job, I'm looking forward to our meeting but only because I need to figure out what she's up to.

As soon as I finish getting ready, I receive text from Alexander.

Good morning. Have I told you how much I love you?

My stomach does a back flip.

You haven't this morning.

A few seconds later, my phone rings.

"Good morning."

"Good morning to you. How are you feeling this morning?"

I groan.

"I'm okay, but unfortunately the apartment complex doesn't have any available units for another six months. So, either I break the contract I just signed or Melanie and I will be neighbors?" I pause, waiting for his response, but he doesn't say anything. I can hear him typing something on his laptop.

"Anyway, I'll figure something out. How are you?"

"Hectic morning, of course. But the reason I'm calling, other than to hear your voice, is to invite you to dinner again, only this time it's at my parents' house. Saturday night—will you be my date?"

Hmm . . . his parents. I've met Penny and Rick once and it was a bit awkward. But only because Alexander had the brilliant idea to *hire* me to redecorate their home as an anniversary gift. Let's just say Penny wasn't too keen on the idea of her son's new girlfriend walking in and changing around the house she's lived in for twenty-something years. Then, there was the whole thing with the menu being straight from the cookbook of Melanie. I didn't feel too confident on the impression I made even though Alexander said it went well.

"I would love to be your date. What's the occasion?"

"No special occasion. I guess Penny's just looking for another excuse to cook."

I grit my teeth.

"Sounds great."

I hold back my sarcastic comment about trying another one of Melanie's extraordinary recipes.

"Are you sure there isn't too much gray?" Valerie asks for the hundredth time. I'm seriously contemplating sticking my pen in my eye, just so I have an excuse to leave. I can't believe this, she picked out all the colors (most of them different shades of gray) and now she's questioning her choices.

"I don't. In fact, I think the schemes work really well together."

Suddenly, a thought pops into my head.

"In fact, I've been looking at a similar color scheme for my new place." I scroll through my files on my laptop. "This is what I was looking at, although now I need to decide if I'm actually going to move."

Valerie gives me a curious look.

"What do you mean? Why wouldn't you move?"

I frown. "Unfortunately, I found out there might be an issue with my apartment. Well, not exactly the apartment, more like a neighbor."

"Oh," Valerie says disappointedly.

It's obvious she's already lost interest, so I know I need to throw out more hints.

"Yeah, I just found out my boyfriend's assistant lives in the building I'm moving into, and unfortunately we don't exactly get along."

And that's all I needed to say to reel her back in.

"You're moving into the same building?"

I nod. "Yes. Can you believe it? What are the chances?"

She chews on her bottom lip. "So, it sounds like you have a complicated relationship with this girl?"

I let out a loud sigh.

"I guess you could say that," I reply. "But, things have been better lately. Hopefully, we've all moved on. And things are really, really amazing with Alexander. I'm a very lucky girl."

Valerie looks as if she's mentally taking notes of everything I say.

"Can I tell you a secret?" I whisper. I don't know why I'm whispering, but it definitely makes me sound more dramatic.

"Yes. Definitely," she replies, more eagerly than I expected.

This is awesome. I'm going to lay it on thick.

"Truthfully, I'm hoping my boyfriend will ask me to move in with him. He's dropped a few subtle hints."

Her eyes grow wide.

"Really? That surprises me that you would want to give up your independence."

What does she mean by that?

"I don't think moving in with him would take away my independence."

She shrugs her shoulders. "I don't know. It sounds like you have a great thing right now. And you don't strike me as the type to let another woman scare you away . . . from the apartment."

And that's all the information I'm going to give her for today.

"I'm so sorry," I exclaim. "Here I am supposed to be decorating your home, and I'm talking about my personal life. That's so unprofessional of me."

She places her hand on mine. "Don't apologize. Just because you're decorating my house doesn't mean we can't be friends. You can talk to me about anything."

Hah. Friends? She's good.

"I appreciate that. It's been difficult lately since my best friend moved to Florida."

She pats my shoulder. "Well, you have me."

I guide her back to discussing her paint selections and off the subject of my personal life. Thankfully, she follows my lead.

On my way home, I start to wonder if Valerie really is up to anything. Maybe I'm completely wrong. Have I become so paranoid that I've let my insecurities control my life? There is one way to find out, and I'm meeting up with her this afternoon. Maybe I should give in and take advantage of having my own personal psychic right downstairs.

Chapter Six

I wonder if I'm getting sick. That's all I need right now. It's either that or I'm having hot flashes from the rising temperatures. Maybe I wouldn't want to live in Florida after all? I sit down on the couch with a cold drink and my laptop while I wait for Mrs. Rothera to come over. I'm just about to send Helena an email when I hear six knocks at my door. Mrs. Rothera always knocks six times.

"Hi," I say cheerfully.

"Hello, Summer," she says. She sounds so formal, so different than usual.

I invite her in and offer her something to drink.

"No thank you."

We sit down at the table, and she produces a few sheets of paper from a manila envelope.

"I'm assuming you're still planning to move at the end of the month?" She glances around the apartment and at my four measly packed boxes in the corner of the room.

I nod slowly. "That's my plan, at least I think so. I just have to figure out how to get past my latest roadblock."

She raises an eyebrow. "Roadblock?"

I let out a loud sigh. "Yes, unfortunately the perfect apartment I found isn't so perfect after all."

She purses her lips. "Oh?"

"This is probably going to sound ridiculous, and I wish it didn't bother me, but I found out that Melanie and I are going to be neighbors. I guess I'm starting to wonder if this is another sign to keep me from moving?"

I can tell she wants to say something.

"Summer, do you want me to tell you what I think?"

I nod. And this time I mean it. I need direction or at least someone to tell me I'm being completely ridiculous.

Her expression turns very serious. "Moving into that apartment is a mistake."

I had a feeling she was going to say that,

"Mrs. Rothera, can I ask you something?"

"Yes," she says, raising one eyebrow.

"Why have you been avoiding me these last few weeks? The last time I was at your apartment you rushed me out without any explanation."

She frowns.

"You aren't going to like hearing this. But, I'm concerned for you."

She's right, I don't want to hear this. In fact, this is exactly what I wanted to avoid.

"I have an uneasy feeling about your move and the negative forces that could affect your happiness. I know how heartbroken you were following your last relationship and . . ."

"Thank you," I interrupt. "I really do appreciate your concern."

She's about to say something else, but she stops.

"It's never going to end, is it?" I ask. "Angie thinks it's time to give Alexander an ultimatum."

Mrs. Rothera is quiet. So quiet that it's starting to scare me.

"I think you need to do whatever will make you happy. Do you know what that is?"

I nod. "I thought I could handle this. But between Helena's warnings and now this new client, who also happens to be good friends with Melanie, it never stops."

"Well, there's your answer."

Crap. I was hoping it wouldn't get to this point.

"Thank you for being a good friend. I'm sorry if I've been difficult."

She laughs.

"You're not the first person to be uncomfortable with my . . . unique qualities."

Now, it's my turn to laugh.

"That's an interesting description."

She shrugs as she stands up. "Anyway, I'll leave you to your work. Just think about what I said before you make your final decision about moving."

"I will."

After she leaves, I stare blankly at my computer screen. I should be working on Helena's dining room, but instead, I'm contemplating how I'm going to break the news to Alexander.

I'm very quiet as we drive to Alexander's parents' house. I've spent the past few days contacting new potential clients that it hasn't given me much time to think (or obsess) about my move or Melanie. Which is probably a good thing.

"Hey. You sure you're okay?" he asks. "Please tell me you aren't worried about seeing my parents again."

I shake my head.

"It's not that. I'm just distracted."

He reaches over and puts his hand on my leg.

"What did you decide about the apartment?"

I groan.

"I have no idea. According to Mrs. Rothera, it would be a very bad idea for me to move in there."

"Are you serious? You're not going to listen to that, are you?"

I stare out the window, and thankfully, we turn onto his parents' street.

"I'm not sure what I'm doing yet."

When he pulls into their long drive, he doesn't turn off the car.

"Summer, I'm worried. You seem distant. Is there something else going on?"

Just then, his father and niece knock on his car window.

"Hi, you two."

Alexander makes a face.

"I would really like to finish this conversation later."

I nod. "Okay."

"I love you."

I give him a grateful smile. "I love you, too."

I really like Alexander's sister Anna. She's friendly and down to earth. She gives me a warm hug as soon as we walk in the house. Which is more than I can say for Penny.

I don't know what it is, but I have a feeling Alexander's mother doesn't care for me.

She's standing over the stove, stirring a big pot of marinara sauce.

"Hello, Summer." She gives me one of those quick cheek kisses. The kind where your cheeks touch and you make a kiss sound.

"Hey, Mom," Alexander says, giving her a hug.

I stand back and watch their interaction. It's very obvious she adores her son. It makes me wonder what kind of relationship she had with Helena?

I can hear Rick playing with Alexander's adorable six-year-old niece Kelsey, and Anna's husband Rob is holding eighteen-month-old Elise.

"Would you two mind setting the table? Oh, and there will be eight of us tonight."

Alexander nods, and then gives her a curious look.

"Eight? There are only seven of us, unless you're planning on allowing Elise to play with your good china."

Penny smiles. "No, I've invited Melanie to join us tonight. She was so helpful with the meal planning for the church banquet last week."

I watch as all the color drains from Alexander's face. He looks in my direction and gives me an apologetic look.

The crazy thing is I'm not surprised Penny invited Melanie —not at all. I have no doubt Melanie has been talking to Penny about me. I'm sure she does it in a very sly and innocent way, because that's what she does.

"Is there a problem?" Penny asks. She must have noticed the awkward silence between Alexander and me.

"No problem at all, Penny," I announce loudly. "Please show me the dishes you would like to use."

Alexander and I follow Penny into her formal dining room, a room that would definitely benefit from a facelift by Summer Interiors. The walls are covered in dated floral print wallpaper, which is peeling in some spots. The cream curtains are faded and dingy. The furniture is very nice, obviously made of good sturdy oak.

"You can use this china," Penny says, opening the cabinet. "The silver is in the drawer."

She rushes back to the kitchen, leaving Alexander and me alone. I don't say anything as I very carefully pull out the good china. The last thing I need to do is break one.

"Sum, I promise I had no idea."

I nod slowly.

"I know you didn't. But I'd say it's obvious that Melanie and your mother have more of a relationship than just sharing recipes."

He drops his head. The last time we discussed this he insisted they just shared recipes from time to time.

"Let's just discuss it later," I whisper. I have a strong feeling there are listening ears from the kitchen.

We set the table in silence, and I head back to the kitchen to help in any way I can.

"Summer. I had a chance to take a look at your website," Anna says with a smile. "You do beautiful work."

I grin widely. "Thank you. I love my job."

At that moment, we're interrupted by a knock at the door. Penny wipes her hands and hurries to answer it. Anna walks by me and squeezes my hand. I give her a grateful smile. As soon as I hear Melanie's voice, I cringe.

"I made the raspberry cheesecake and a turtle cheesecake. Since that's Alexander's favorite."

"You're wonderful. Thank you," Penny gushes.

I awkwardly lean on the counter when they join us in the kitchen.

"Hi, everyone," Melanie says.

Anna, Alexander, and I all say hello at the same time. Melanie immediately starts discussing work with Alexander, going out of her way to ignore my presence.

I stand awkwardly off to the side, feeling completely out of place. I can't help but wonder how I got to this point? The truth is it's partly my fault, because I allowed this to go on. Helena is right. Angie is right. I don't want to wake up years down the road with this other person affecting my relationship.

"Okay, everyone to the dining room," Penny shouts, dragging me out of my thoughts.

Alexander puts his arm around me and guides me to the dining room. I look around and a thought crosses my mind. I guess this is how it will always be, one big happy family that obviously includes Melanie.

Chapter Seven

The dinner is uneventful other than Kelsey's temper tantrum about wanting to hold a knife and cut her dinner roll. Alexander and Melanie are deep in conversation about the recent events within their company. I remain mostly quiet, picking at my food.

"Melanie, before I forget, please thank your friend Valerie for that pastry chef recommendation," Penny says. "The desserts were a huge hit at the banquet."

Thanks to Penny, I finally have the answer I've been hoping for since the day I heard Valerie whispering on the phone. It's at this exact moment everything comes crashing down —for Melanie.

"Valerie? As in Valerie Watson?" I interrupt, raising my voice to a level that probably isn't suitable for one of Penny's dinners.

Penny, Alexander, and Melanie all look at me. I guess I was yelling or maybe they're looking at me because it's the first time I've spoken a word since we sat down at the table.

Melanie's eyes grow wide. "Um, yes."

"Summer, do you know Valerie?" Penny asks.

I glare at Melanie. She makes every effort to avoid making eye contact with me, even pretending to choke on her wine.

"I do know Valerie. In fact, she just hired me to decorate her home."

"What a small world?" Penny says, as she folds her napkin into a small square.

"It really is," I say. My tone is so sarcastic I have no doubt Alexander has caught on. "Valerie told me she was referred through a friend. Was that you, Melanie?"

I look at Alexander out of the corner of my eye. He's watching our conversation intently. I think I see a few beads of sweat on his forehead.

Melanie shifts around in her chair. All eyes are on her now.

"Oh, um, I didn't realize you were decorating her house," she stutters. Ha! There's no way for her to escape this conversation, except maybe a sudden bathroom emergency.

I fold my arms.

"Really? Alexander says you two are good friends. You really had no idea I was her decorator?"

I watch as Melanie continues to squirm.

"You know, I think I did mention you had decorated Alexander's home—and did a fantastic job."

I force a smile.

"Well, I should be thanking you then . . . for the referral."

Melanie nods as everyone else at the table sits quietly, listening to our conversation. The only sound is coming from Kelsey's iPad.

"You're welcome, but I don't know that I did anything," she says, fumbling over her words.

I look at Alexander once again, hoping he will say something.

"Penny, let me help you with the dishes," Melanie exclaims, finally finding the perfect excuse to end our conversation. She's been caught, and she knows it.

She and Penny pick up several dishes and head off to the kitchen.

"Summer, would you like to help me get Elise changed?" Anna asks. I could kiss her right now. And yes, I would rather change a toddler's dirty diaper than wash dishes with Melanie any day.

Alexander joins Rick and Rob in their discussion about preseason football, although he looks slightly nauseous.

A few minutes later, I'm standing next to Anna as she gently lays Elise on the bed in Penny's bright yellow guest room.

"Are you okay?"

I let out a loud sigh. I feel very comfortable with Anna, so it doesn't surprise me when I suddenly unload all my pent-up frustration.

"I don't know if I can do this—deal with Melanie, not change the baby."

She smiles. "I know what you were referring to."

"I really thought I could," I continue, as I rub my temples. "I respect Alexander and his career, but I can't go on like this."

I decide to tell her about what I overheard when Valerie was on the phone.

"So, what do you think is the purpose of Valerie hiring you?" she asks.

I shrug. "I'm not exactly sure. Maybe it's some diabolical plan to sabotage my business? Or maybe she's planning on accusing me of something horrible, anything to break up Alexander and me. According to Helena, Melanie's capable of anything."

She raises her eyebrows. "So, you've met Helena?"

I roll my eyes. "Oh yeah, I'm actually redecorating her apartment."

Anna throws her head back in laughter.

"I'm sorry I'm laughing. Being with my kids all the time, I don't get this kind of excitement often."

I can't help but laugh as well.

"Seriously, I couldn't make this stuff up if I tried. My best friend, Angie, says she doesn't understand how I get myself into these messes, but here I am."

Anna puts a pair of Minnie Mouse pajamas on Elise, while making faces at her. Elise giggles in delight.

"Speaking of Helena? Did you all get along with her?"

I've been dying to know what Alexander's family thought of Helena and their divorce.

Anna makes a face. "We didn't see much of them during their marriage, but when we did she was always pleasant. Not overly warm, but pleasant. I just don't believe she ever had any desire to be a part of this family."

Hmmm . . . this is interesting.

"Well, according to her, Melanie was a major factor in their marriage breaking up."

She nods as if she already knew that.

"I'm sure she was. Melanie's involvement in Alexander's life is not an ideal situation. I would *never* tolerate Rob having an assistant who's so immersed in our personal lives. So, I can see where you're coming from." She pauses, picking up Elise. "And as far as my mother, it's nothing personal toward you. She and Melanie have similar interests, especially with the cooking thing. Helena never really made an effort to form a bond with her and I believe Mom always wanted that with the woman Alexander ended up with."

"Everything all right in here?" Alexander interrupts.

Anna and I glance at each other.

"I'll let you two talk." She hurries out of the room with Elise over her shoulder.

I make myself busy folding the baby blankets Anna left in the room. Alexander and I are silent for a few seconds. I'm not sure what it is, but something feels different between us and I don't like it.

"Summer, I'm so sorry about everything that happened at dinner. There has to be some kind of explanation for Valerie. Summer Interiors is becoming quite popular so . . ."

"What?" I interrupt, raising my voice once again. "Alexander, do you hear yourself? Why can't you just admit that Melanie is purposely trying to cause problems? She couldn't even explain her connection to Valerie. If that isn't a red flag, then I don't know what is."

He stares at the floor.

"And you don't think it's odd that she accepted a dinner invitation tonight knowing we would be here too?"

Silence.

I need to get the hell out of here.

"I'm ready to go home."

"Summer . . ."

"I want to go home," I reply calmly.

The next few minutes happen so quickly I feel like I'm outside of my body watching it. I quickly gather my things and say my good-byes to Alexander's family, giving them the ever-convenient excuse that I don't feel well. Anna gives me a tight hug while Penny offers me an aspirin.

I glance at Melanie before we leave. I contemplate the ways I could wipe the smug expression off her face. Instead, I walk out without saying a word to her. Unfortunately, she may succeed in doing what she's wanted since the first day I showed up to decorate Alexander's home. I know what I need to do now, and I can already feel my heart breaking even worse than it did last summer when Jake left me alone on the beach.

I silently stare out the window as we make our way back to my apartment. My mind is racing with hundreds of different thoughts. Thankfully, Alexander respects the fact that I don't want to talk right now. I will have plenty to say to him soon enough.

I know I've finally reached my breaking point. I wonder if this is how Helena felt. The only difference is she walked away from a marriage of four years . . . and what some of her friends say, the greatest love story of all time. Gag.

We almost make it back to my apartment when Alexander breaks the horrible silence in the car. The tension is so thick I contemplate opening my window.

"Please talk to me."

I take a deep breath. "What do you want me to say? Do you want me to tell you I'll just stand back while you have another discussion with Melanie? Are you going to threaten her to stay out of our lives again? Or are you going to tell me that Melanie and your mother barely know each other, when it's obvious they have more of a relationship than you thought?" I pause, before continuing with my monologue. "Is tonight an example of how dinners with your family are going to always be? I thought I could handle being your girlfriend while you have this assistant so involved in almost every aspect of your life. It's just not going to work . . . so . . ." I take a deep breath as I fight back the tears. "It's time for you to choose—Melanie or me?"

As hard as I was trying to fight back the tears, they make their way out of my eyes and down my cheeks. I know I'm making the right decision. I love Alexander, but I also know that I will never be completely happy if things continue the way they are. I would hate to be years into our relationship and this situation slowly destroy us as it did with Helena.

Alexander is gripping the steering wheel so tightly that his knuckles are turning white. He slowly pulls up in front of my apartment building and puts the car into park. The tears are still rolling down my cheeks, but I'm not sobbing. I'm surprisingly calm despite the huge rock in the pit of my stomach.

"Please don't do this," he says, his voice barely over a whisper. "I don't want to lose you or lose what we have."

I wipe my cheeks with both my hands.

I look at his face for the first the time since we left his parents' house. His normally confident exterior is gone, and he looks completely distraught. I wouldn't be surprised if he started crying along with me. Once again, I begin to doubt this decision. Maybe I'm the one being inconsiderate, insecure, and selfish? I close my eyes and suddenly I feel as if a slide show of the past ten months begins to play for me. I can see Melanie interrupting our close moments, the nonstop phone calls, plotting with Jake to break us up, telling Mrs. Rothera about my decision to move, convincing Valerie to hire me, and antagonizing me about her relationship with Penny and Alexander's family.

Of course, Helena's words begin repeating in my mind. Melanie destroyed their marriage of four years; she's capable of anything. At least I can say I made an effort in the beginning, and I was willing to coexist with her in Alexander's life.

Alexander grabs my hand and holds on to it for dear life.

"I will do whatever it takes to show you that you come first in my life. In fact, I was . . ." He inhales deeply. "I was going to ask you to move in with me, especially since you've hit so many obstacles with your moving plans. I'm ready to take the next step with you and really begin our life together."

He hasn't let go of my hand, and the truth is I don't want him to let go of it—ever. And I would love nothing more than to take the next step in our relationship. Not to mention it would solve a lot of issues for me. But, moving in with him isn't going to solve the biggest issue in our relationship.

"I wish that was enough," I say softly. "But us living together won't fix the way we disagree about Melanie and her constant presence in our lives. And it really concerns me that you can't see the effect she's had on your life. She destroyed your marriage."

He shakes his head. "That's not entirely true. Helena and I rushed into our marriage; we barely knew each other even when we were married. It wasn't going to last with or without Melanie."

I purse my lips. "Okay, but you can't tell me she had *nothing* to do with your issues."

"Oh no, she did."

"Do you see what I'm saying? I'm not willing to risk it. I don't want to be years into our relationship and still arguing over this."

He nods. "Okay."

I'm not sure what he means by okay. Okay—as in he agrees? Okay—as in he chooses me? Or okay—as in he's letting me go? The rock in my stomach seems to be growing and I start to feel like I can't breathe. I grab my bag, throw the car door open, and take off running toward my apartment.

"Summer," Alexander yells, jumping out of the car.

The tears are falling again, and just as I reach my building, the door flies open and Mrs. Rothera appears with her arms outstretched. Without thinking, I run into her arms and begin sobbing on her shoulder.

"Summer," Alexander calls again, finally catching up to me.

"Just give her some space," Mrs. Rothera says softly. "Go home and think about everything. You two can talk in the morning."

"But, I have to . . ."

"Go home and decide," she tells him.

I unwind myself from her arms and run into the building, not looking back at Alexander. I've made my decision, now it's time for him to make his.

Chapter Eight

I don't usually binge on anything. In fact, I'm pretty healthy overall, but for some reason, relationship drama turns me into a raging sugar addict. Last summer, when Jake dumped me and left me at the beach, I ate my way through several boxes of Little Debbie Swiss Cake Rolls thanks to Angie's endless stash of junk food.

Unfortunately, Angie's no longer here, so I have to settle for the stale Oreos in my pantry. I'm sure I look completely pathetic right now with my tear-stained face, hugging the package of cookies as if my life depended on it. I'm so thankful Mrs. Rothera hasn't knocked on my door wanting to talk. I hope she takes her own advice and leaves me alone.

After I calm down, I curl up on the couch and replay the last few minutes with Alexander. The worst part is that even after everything I said to him, he still couldn't tell me he would choose me. I guess that should tell me something. I look out the window to see if by some crazy chance he's still out there, but he's gone. My mind begins to wander again . . . did I make the right decision or did I just destroy the best thing that's ever happened to me? A few seconds later, there's a knock at my door. I don't need to be a psychic to know who it is.

"Be right there," I call.

I quickly throw away the now empty package of Oreos and grab a paper towel to wipe my face. I open the door to find Mrs. Rothera holding a tray. I smell peppermint, so I'm sure it's something to calm me down. And who knows what else she put in there? I know how crazy this sounds, but there have a been a few occasions when I thought Mrs. Rothera was mixing magic potions.

"I'm sorry to bother you. I just wanted to drop this off. It's tea, a calming blend, perfect to help you relax and get some sleep."

Ha, I knew it.

"Thanks," I say, eyeing the teapot with caution.

She's staring at me, which is making me nervous.

"Um, if you don't mind, I kind of want to be alone."

She nods her head slowly, and I get the feeling she's not surprised by the events of tonight.

"I understand."

She turns and starts to walk away.

"Wait," I yell.

She stops dead in her tracks as if she was expecting me to stop her.

"Actually, I'd like you to come in."

She follows me into my apartment. I place the tray of magic tea down on the table. I have no intention of ingesting her crazy concoction.

"I suppose you know what happened with Alexander."

She fidgets with her rings.

"I don't know the exact details, but I have a pretty good idea."

I chew on my bottom lip.

"I finally told Alexander he needed to choose between Melanie and me." I try to swallow the lump in my throat. Unfortunately, once again I fail at holding back the tears. "Anyway, I guess it was just a matter of time," I say, through my tears. "It's obvious he's not ready to let her go from his life."

I wasn't planning to unload all my emotional turmoil on Mrs. Rothera. I was saving that for a phone call to Angie.

"You need to believe that everything will work out the way it's supposed to. The universe will bring you the life you're meant to have."

I appreciate her trying to help, but this is not what I want to hear right now. What I want is for her to tell me that Alexander will realize what needs to be done. Honestly, is it really that difficult to find a new assistant? I know Melanie does a great job and she knows his business inside out, but I'm sure life would go on without her.

"She's getting exactly what she wanted all along," I wail. "Remember when she came to see you for advice and you told her she wouldn't have a future with Alexander?"

She looks at the floor. "Summer, I haven't been completely honest with you."

My heart sinks into my stomach. Those are some of the worst words anyone can say, other than "it's over" or "let's just be friends." Either way, I know I'm not going to like what she's about to say.

"Okay."

She clears her throat.

"Even though I *believe* there's no future for Melanie and Alexander, I still encouraged her to go after what she wanted. It wouldn't be fair of me not to, and I thought she would give up as time went on and your relationship with him grew deeper."

I don't respond to her admission because I just don't know what to say. Yes, I would have hoped she would be on my side, but I haven't exactly taken any of her advice seriously, so I should never have assumed she had my back.

"There's something else."

Seriously? What a way to kick me when I'm down.

"It's not a secret that I don't want you to move."

Ha. The only way it would be less of a secret is if she was shouting it from the roof.

"I know you don't, but I've given you plenty of time to find a new tenant."

She shakes her head. "Do you think this is about rent money?"

I'm confused. "Yeah."

"It's never been about the money." She looks down at her hands, now neatly folded in her lap. "The truth is I'm very lonely. I've enjoyed having you here. And that's also why I hired you to decorate my apartment, and why I changed my mind on décor so many times."

Ahhh . . . this is all starting to make sense.

"I knew you weren't going to stay forever, but I was hoping you would stay a little while longer, so I . . . I helped Melanie come up with a plan to cause some issues for you. I thought if you were having trouble in your business you may not want to have the stress of moving on top of everything."

Whoa. I'm completing dumbfounded right now. Is she for real?

"What do you mean you came up with a plan?"

Before she can respond, I figure it out for myself.

"Valerie."

She hangs her head. "I'm so embarrassed."

"What exactly was going to happen with this plan?" I ask through my gritted teeth. All my tears are gone, and I can actually feel my blood pressure rising by the second.

She lets out a huge sigh. "Melanie came to me desperate for advice. She's so head over heels in love with Alexander, and she's still holding out hope that things will finally happen for them. In her mind, she can do and say anything and he still won't let her go. She believes the reason he won't let her go is because he has feelings for her deep down."

I put my face in my hands. Nothing would surprise me at this point. Maybe he does have feelings for her.

Mrs. Rothera continues talking. "Melanie wanted your attention on something other than Alexander, and I wanted your attention on something other than moving. I know how important your work is to you, so we thought . . ."

"Hold on," I say, putting my hand up. "*You* were going to sabotage my business?"

She looks horrified that I would suggest such a thing. "No, not at all. We just wanted to distract you."

This is the most insane thing I've ever heard. I was right all along about Valerie, and I was right about that phone call.

And the worst part is that no matter what I say, I don't think Alexander would believe me.

One thing's for sure, I would have never thought that Mrs. Rothera would go along with something like this.

"Can you please go?" I say calmly.

I don't know if I'm technically allowed to kick my landlord out of my apartment, but considering this new information, I feel it's justified.

"I truly am sorry," she says, hanging her head.

"Please go. I can't handle any more of this tonight."

She makes her way toward the door but stops before she leaves.

"For what it's worth, Alexander does love you and you could have a beautiful life together."

I close the door behind her. First of all, I don't believe anything she says, and if Alexander loves me as much as he says, he would respect me enough to take my feelings into account.

And after tonight, I don't have faith that's going to happen.

Chapter Nine

"What the hell is going on? I move away and everything falls apart," Angie yells. It's one o'clock in the morning when she finally returns my calls. Yes, calls, as in many urgent calls.

"So, are you two officially broken up?"

I sigh. "I don't know what we are. I finally took your advice and gave him an ultimatum, but I was so emotional that I didn't even give him a chance to talk. He did ask me to move in with him, though."

"What?" she yells (this time she's actually yelling).

I tell her about our conversation.

"I knew it. He's wanted you to move in with him this whole time."

I rub my eyes. I'm so emotionally drained from this night, but I know I won't be able to get any sleep.

"Yeah. But when I asked him to choose between us, he just avoided it. He's not ready to give her up, and I don't want to share him anymore, so I'm not sure where that leaves us. Moving in together is the worst thing that could happen."

I begin to cry once again.

"Oh, Sum, I'm so sorry I'm not there."

"I know." I blow my nose loudly.

"Maybe you need to get away for a few days," Angie exclaims. "When's the last time you took some time off?"

I dab the corner of my eyes. "Um, that would be last summer when we were all at the beach."

"Oh."

"Yep. And we all know how that vacation ended." I pause. "Alexander and I were just talking about taking a trip. That's definitely not happening any time soon."

Angie is quiet, which doesn't happen often.

"Ang, you still there?"

"Yes, I was just thinking—why don't you come here for a few days, just to clear your head? A few days on a Florida beach can do wonders."

That doesn't sound like a bad idea. I'm at a good place with my clients and getting away from everything and everyone sounds pretty great.

"Summer."

"I'll do it. I will look at flights tonight. A few days in Florida are exactly what I need."

After getting off the phone with Angie, I book a flight to Florida for next weekend. I wouldn't normally just take off, but I know I need this. Despite minimal sleep, I make sure I'm out of my apartment as soon as the sun comes up. I have no interest in seeing Mrs. Rothera this morning. It's actually a beautiful summer morning, so I sit outside at my favorite café with a coffee and my laptop.

Before making any more travel plans, I follow up on an order for Helena and send her a text letting her know I will be out of town for a few days. Now, if only I can figure out how to handle this situation with Valerie. I don't know whether I should confront her or just fire myself as her decorator. Honestly, I wonder how far she was going to take her act. I suppose I should have caught on sooner when she changed her mind on everything she chose. I feel so stupid.

I lean back in my chair and take a sip of my first cup of coffee. I have no doubt I will need more than one cup to make it through the day after maybe three hours of sleep. I haven't heard a word from Alexander since I asked him to leave last night, and I'm not sure if that's good or bad. In a perfect world, he's letting Melanie go right this second.

I must be so deep in thought I don't notice someone calling

my name. Either that or I'm beyond exhausted and have fallen asleep with my eyes open.

"Summer."

I look up from my laptop to see Jake standing next to me. He's wearing a tight Adidas shirt, running shorts, and a baseball cap. I can't deny that I still find him physically attractive.

"Summer," he repeats. "You okay?"

"What? Oh yeah, I just didn't get much sleep last night."

He sits down on the edge of the chair across from me. Huh, that's funny because I don't remember inviting him to sit with me. Unless I was asleep . . .

"Do you mind if I sit?"

He must have read my mind.

"I have a lot of work to get done," I say, pretending to open a file on my laptop.

He gives me a curious look. "You sure you're okay?"

"Yep. Just a lot going on before I leave town for a few days. So, if you don't mind . . ."

He doesn't move from his chair, obviously not taking my hint.

"Jake, what do you want?"

He puts both hands around his coffee cup and tightens his lips.

"What do I want? That's a loaded question."

Crap. I totally walked into this one.

"Actually, I've had a lot of time to think about this the past few months. And what I want the most is for you to be happy." He stops and takes a deep breath. "I made the biggest mistake of my life last summer, and I regret it more than you know. But, you deserve better than me, you deserve to be treated like you're the most important person in the universe. I failed at that, and I don't blame you for not taking me back."

Wow. For the first time since last summer I believe he has remorse for hurting me like he did.

He stands up from the chair and picks up his coffee. "Make sure Alexander takes good care of you."

He's about to walk away, but I stop him.

"Thank you, Jake. I hope you find whatever it is you're looking for."

He smiles. "Me, too."

After he leaves, I think about one of the things he said. I do deserve to be treated like the most important person in the world. And because of this, I know I made the right decision by asking Alexander to choose. The truth is it's not fair to Melanie or me if our situation continues this way.

Surprisingly, I'm glad I saw Jake. This was the closure I've been looking for since we broke up. I do wish him happiness despite how much he hurt me, and I know I can't let that hurt define my future.

~

"I want to go with you," Gina wails.

I giggle. "Really? Do you really think you will be able to pry yourself away from Vinny for an entire weekend?"

She scowls.

"What's that supposed to mean? Of course I can."

I raise my eyebrows because I can't remember the last time I saw her, and I know she's been spending her every waking moment with Vinny.

"Don't get defensive. You're welcome to come if you want."

She folds her arms. I know she won't go through with it unless Vinny joins her. Of course, Angie and Vinny are cousins so he just may. Great. And then it will be me with the two happy couples. Ugh.

"I knew that girl was trouble since day one. You just let me know and we can get that problem taken care of, if you know what I mean."

I laugh. Of course I know what she means.

"Thanks, I'll let you know."

"And what about that landlord of yours? We might as well take care of her, too."

I force a smile.

"I appreciate it, Gina." I pause. "I do need your help with something, though. I need to find a place to live. I cancelled my contract at the new complex. There was no way in hell I was going to live in the same building as Melanie."

She gives me a thoughtful look. "You could stay with me, it would be tight but . . ."

"Thanks, girl, but your tiny studio is definitely not big enough for both of us."

This is a nice way of telling her I would never live with her. Not only is her place the size of a shoebox, but also she's a complete slob.

"Does Alexander know you're taking a trip?"

I shake my head.

"No. I haven't spoken to him since I asked him to leave last night."

Gina's face softens from her normally tough exterior, and she pats my shoulder.

"Don't worry about it. He'll do the right thing."

I shrug my shoulders.

"I saw Jake earlier today. He said something that got me thinking."

Gina's eyes grow wide. "No way. Don't you dare think about it," she demands.

I laugh. "Very funny. Don't worry, we're not getting back together. In fact, I think we both finally got the closure we needed."

Relief washes over her face. "Oh good. Don't scare me like that. What exactly did Jake say? He doesn't exactly exude eloquence."

I snort. Gina has never been a Jake fan.

"He told me he wanted me to be happy and that I should be treated like the most important person in the universe. That just reminded me that I don't feel that way when Melanie is in the picture."

She frowns. "Well, as much as I hate to agree with anything that comes out of Jake's mouth, he has a point."

"Yes, he does . . . believe it or not, I actually feel better after talking to him."

Gina begins to make gagging noises.

"At least he didn't mention your *amazing* decorating magic and try to manipulate you into giving him another chance."

I roll my eyes. Jake used to tell everyone that I had some kind of decorating magic. Gina thought it was annoying, and she continues to bring it up to this day.

"Nope. I believe that chapter is finally closed. We're both moving on once and for all."

Chapter Ten

This may be the longest I've gone without talking to Alexander since the day we met. It's been three long days since the horrific dinner at his parents' house. I've managed to avoid him, which has been absolute torture because I miss him so much. He's tried calling and has texted several times. Of course, none of his texts mention my ultimatum. Even though it's been hard, I'm proud of myself for staying strong. I keep reminding myself that until he makes up his mind I have nothing to say to him.

In each message, he tells me how much he loves me and that we will get past this. This morning he left me a message about having to go to Boston for two days, but he wants to talk when he gets back, the same day I leave for Florida.

My trip to Florida is the only bright spot in my life right now, and I'm counting the minutes until my escape from reality. I've also managed to avoid all contact with Mrs.

Rothera by staying late at my office, going to the mall, and going to Starbucks. Basically, anything that will keep me out past her bedtime. The good news is I'm hopeful I will be out of this mess sooner than I expected. Gina has a friend who's looking for someone to rent her house. I've already set up a time to meet her when I return from my trip.

In the meantime, I'm completely dreading my meeting this morning with Valerie.

I'm sure she's spoken to Melanie by now, but she didn't mention it when I asked to meet. My plan is to just come out and confront her. I'm hoping she tells me the truth, but I'm not going to hold my breath. Anyway, it really doesn't matter because I have a feeling she's no longer going to be a client an hour from now.

As soon as I arrive I know something's different. She seems more relaxed than she usually is. Unfortunately, we're not alone—Melanie is sitting at the kitchen table, ready to pounce. Normally, this would throw me off but not today. I think deep down I had a feeling something like this would happen.

"Hello, Melanie," I say formally.

"Summer."

I look back and forth between the two of them, waiting for someone to break the ice.

"Summer, I'm glad you asked to meet today because I

wanted to talk to you," Valerie says, being the first to break the tension.

"I asked Melanie here so we could all discuss and get everything out in the open."

I glance at Melanie who's trying very hard to pretend she cares, but she's doing a crappy job.

Valerie sits down at the table next to Melanie. I'm still standing—just in case I have to make a quick getaway.

"I know what you must be thinking," Valerie starts.

"Do you?" I interrupt. "I'm surprised you don't want to wait for your third conspirator. Shouldn't Mrs. Rothera be here?"

Both women look completely shocked. I'm not sure if they're shocked I called them out or shocked that I know she was in on this, too.

"But please, let's *discuss* why it is you hired me and what your grand plan really was."

I pull out one of the chairs and sit down with a sudden unexpected burst of confidence.

Valerie looks to Melanie for advice.

"Oh come on, Melanie, please tell me. I can't believe you're so desperate that you would resort to something so ridiculous—but wait, that's your style, right? Didn't I hear that you even fabricated some photos to break up Alexander and Helena?"

If looks could kill, I'm sure I would be dead and buried right now.

"I don't have any idea what you're talking about. It sounds like you're listening to that awful Helena again. I guess it's true—you know, that saying about a women scorned." She shakes her head. "Helena blames me for their marriage breaking up, but the truth is she only has herself to blame."

It's my turn to glare at her.

"Really? But it worked in your favor. With Helena out of the picture you had Alexander all to yourself." I stop and give her my most sweet and innocent smile. "That is until I came along."

Valerie's looking back and forth between us—I wouldn't be surprised if she made a bag of popcorn to go along with the show she's getting.

Melanie starts laughing. "Yes, you came along—a quick replacement for that self-absorbed, cold bitch he was married to. The funny thing is I'm still here, too. I was there when he and Helena broke up, and I will be here when you two break up."

It takes all my strength not to lose my cool. I want more than anything to tell her that's never going to happen, but I don't know that. Instead, I ignore her and look at Valerie.

"Well, I'm assuming this means our partnership is over. Although, it wasn't really a partnership, was it? The complaints about gray paint colors and finding the perfect wall mirror were all part of this ridiculous idea. I give you credit, though, you had me completely fooled."

She shrugs, not able to look me in the eye. I have a feeling she does feel some kind of remorse despite being besties with Melanie.

"I will tear up the contracts and considering the um . . . situation . . ."—I give Melanie a side-glance—"I won't take legal action because I'd rather be done with all of this nonsense."

I grab my bag and make my way toward the door. I stop and turn around.

"I'll be sure to let Alexander know how unfortunate it is that we're no longer working together."

I leave before Melanie can twist the knife any further in my back. The fact is she's absolutely right about her being in Alexander's life and there isn't a damn thing I can do about it. Unfortunately, I just have to wait for him to finally make his choice.

"When are you coming back? You are coming back, aren't you?" Helena asks, raising her voice slightly. I'm not sure why she's so concerned with me leaving because getting in touch with her on most days has proven to be an act of congress. This may go down in history as one of the longest projects ever.

"Of course I'm coming back. I just need a few days away."

I'm standing in front of my closet, looking at the many items hanging in front of me and still wondering why I have nothing to pack.

"Is Xander going along on this holiday?"

I cringe.

"No, he's not. His work is keeping him busy." That's the easiest answer. I'd rather not discuss my relationship issues with my boyfriend's ex-wife. Seriously, I feel like I'm living on a trashy talk show.

"Yes. It always does. You might as well get used to it."

"Mmmhmm. Anyway, I just wanted to let you know. I will touch base with you again when I return."

After we hang up I continue to look through my clothes, mainly because I need to pack but also because I need a distraction. Angie says it's too hot to function right now, so I decide on a few dresses, swimsuits, and some shorts. I neatly roll my clothes and place them strategically in my carry-on suitcase.

As I look around my apartment, it occurs to me that it was almost a year ago I was packing for my beach trip with Jake. I remember being so excited to spend that time with him; of course, I had no idea what was about to happen. I remember I had just finished redecorating his boss's summerhouse and I was on top of the world. Everything was perfect and just like that—poof—eighteen months was gone in an instant. I suppose I should have expected something to happen; nothing in life is ever that perfect.

This is different, though. The way I love Alexander, these feelings are so much deeper than what I felt for Jake. When we're together, it feels like all the puzzle pieces in my life fit perfectly. Which makes this time apart even harder. "Ugh. Snap out of it, Summer," I scold. I refuse to second-guess myself anymore. I deserve to be number one in his life, and if he can't make me that—well, then perhaps the puzzle doesn't fit as perfectly as I thought.

Chapter Eleven

*F*inally. I've never been more ready for a vacation in my life. I'm just about to walk out the door to my awaiting cab when Mrs. Rothera appears at my doorway. Not even she can ruin my good mood. She looks down at my suitcase and back up to my wide-brimmed straw hat.

"Where are you off to?"

Shouldn't she already know the answer, you know, being a psychic and all?

"I'm going to see Angie."

Relief washes over her face. Maybe she thought I was trying to sneak out. Honestly, the thought has crossed my mind.

"That will be nice. Please give her my best."

"Sure," I say nonchalantly.

She clears her throat. "I'm glad I saw you before you left. I've been trying to catch up with you but . . ."

"I've been busy," I interrupt. I look in my bag to make sure I have everything.

"My cab is waiting, so if you'll excuse me."

I double-check the lock and rush out toward the cab. Mrs. Rothera follows me, practically running alongside me.

"I wanted to tell you something . . . and I think you may be happy about it."

The cab driver puts my suitcase in the trunk.

"You know what," I snap. "I don't need anyone to tell me what's going to make me happy. I've decided that I can make my own happiness, whether that includes Alexander or not."

I climb into the cab.

"But it's about your move."

"Good-bye, Mrs. Rothera." I close the car door, not giving her a chance to tell me what she wanted.

I lean my head against the seat as we make our way toward the airport. I'm not going to lie, I'm curious about what she wanted to tell me. But, I also don't want anything to ruin my trip. I don't want to talk about my move or Melanie or even Alexander. I just want to relax on a beach far away from my life and all the stress that goes along with it.

∼

"You've lost weight," Angie yells as soon as she sees me. "Are you eating, because it doesn't look like you've had a good bowl of pasta since I left."

I notice several people looking at us in the middle of the airport terminal.

"Ha-ha. Of course I'm eating."

She gives me a skeptical look.

"I'm so happy you're here," she shouts, engulfing me in a huge hug.

We both squeal like a couple of teenagers.

Angie is talking a mile a minute as she rushes out of the airport. I'm breaking a sweat trying to keep up with her. As soon as we exit, the humidity hits me. Holy crap. Don't get me wrong, it can get humid in Connecticut, but it's like a sauna out here.

"Wow. You weren't kidding about the heat."

She laughs.

"It's summertime in Florida, what else were you expecting?"

I can't believe I'm here. I look out the window at the blue skies and the palm trees. Maybe I could live here? It's hot as hell outside, but the idea of no more brutal winters is promising.

The plan is to stay at Angie's house in Orlando tonight, and then head to the beach tomorrow. Honestly, I don't care what we do. I'm just so happy to be here.

I haven't laughed this hard in months. It's been so awesome just catching up and reminiscing with Angie. I really miss this.

"Too bad Gina isn't here," Angie says, dragging me out of my thoughts. "She'd have plenty of stories to share."

I laugh. "Yeah. She told me she wanted to come, but I don't think she could be away from Vinny that long. To tell you the truth, I was a little worried that she was going to bring him. I really didn't want to be stuck with two happy couples all weekend."

She shakes her head. "No need to worry about that. This is a girls only weekend, which is why I banished Brett from the house tonight."

I give her a grateful smile, which quickly turns to a frown.

"Oh, Ang, did I mess everything up with Alexander? Deep down, I know it was time to stand up for myself, but I haven't given Alexander a chance to explain since it all went down. Maybe I should . . ."

"Don't," she interrupts. "You did the right thing and Alexander will realize that."

The familiar feeling of dread has returned. I was hoping to keep this feeling away from invading my trip but no such luck.

"Enough about that," Angie yells. "We probably should turn in. We have to be up early in the morning for our massages."

"Massages?"

She smiles.

"Yep. My treat."

I don't know what I did to get such an awesome friend, but I couldn't be more thankful for her than I am right now.

I need to move to the beach. I feel like a completely different person than I did yesterday. It could be the amazing massage I had this morning, or it could be the fact that I'm sitting on a balcony of our hotel room listening to the waves. I've only been here a few hours, but I'm beginning to feel like my old self. The confident happy woman I used to be before I let other people affect me. Angie rented us a two-bedroom suite and it's completely amazing. I offered to split the bill with her but she went completely ballistic on me. I'm just glad I won't be around when she gets her credit card statement next month.

Angie decided she needed to take a nap, which is funny because we haven't done anything other than lie around all morning. I take this opportunity to catch up on some emails. I know I'm not supposed to be working, but I can't unplug completely when I have my own business.

The first email I see is from Chantel, another referral from Alexander. She's ready to meet to discuss my upcoming project decorating her home. This is a huge relief, especially after the whole Valerie disaster, and since I'm obviously down one client I will need the business. And I'm sure Helena's apartment is going to drag out until the end of time.

The second email is from Gina's friend, confirming our meeting to look at her house. I reply immediately with a "Yes, definitely." I manage to stop myself from responding in all caps, not wanting to look completely desperate (which I am).

"What are you doing?" Angie yells, startling me.

"Crap. You scared me," I shout. "I thought you were taking a nap."

She furrows her brow. "And you're supposed to be on vacation. That means no emails and no work."

I quickly close my laptop. "I am, but I had to check in—I'm done."

She sits down. "I have a surprise for you."

I give her a worried look. "Another one? I appreciate it, Ang, but you're going into major debt from this weekend. Please let me pay for something."

She laughs. "I'm not spending any money on this surprise. Someone is on their way to crash our weekend."

I can feel my pulse pick up and for a second all I can think about is Alexander.

"He's coming," I exclaim.

She looks confused.

"He? No. It's Gina. She just called to find out where we are. She and Vinny flew in this morning, but don't worry, he's staying with Brett. No boys are allowed here."

I can feel my heart sink, but I do my best to recover and hide my disappointment. Having Gina here will be awesome.

"Did you think Alexander was coming?"

I shrug and turn back to face the ocean.

"Summer?"

"For a second I did." I swallow hard to try to get rid of the lump that's returned in my throat. "Or I was hoping at least. I guess I'm feeling guilty because I haven't returned any of his calls. I didn't even tell him I was coming here."

"Maybe you *should* call him or at least text him," she says.

I turn back to face her.

"What do I say?"

She puts her arm around my shoulder.

"Just tell him you came to visit me and you're willing to talk when you get back. You don't have to say anything else."

She's right.

I reach for my phone and make my way to my room. I start to type a text but erase it about ten times before sending.

> *Thanks for your messages. I'm in Florida with Angie. Let's talk when I return.*

Ugh. I sound so formal.

I'm about to send another text when he texts me back.

> *There's nothing more to say. I'm tired of trying. It's over.*

I stare blankly at my phone, suddenly feeling dizzy. I sit down on the bed before I pass out.

I'm too late. He's tried contacting me several times and I've ignored him, not even giving him a chance to explain. Giving him an ultimatum wasn't enough; I've pushed him further away and quite possibly into Melanie's waiting arms.

"Gina should be here in about an hour. How about we . . ." Angie stops and stares at me. "What happened?"

I can't even speak, so I hand her my phone.

"It's over," I say, my voice barely over a whisper.

Those are the only words I can say before collapsing into the ugly cry. Maybe this is a sign I should avoid the beach in the summertime. Heartbreak two years in a row is more than enough.

Chapter Twelve

_T_he sunlight is pouring into my bedroom, it's so bright that I cover my eyes with my arm. I can totally hear Gina and Angie talking in the living room. It's not like Angie could ever whisper anyway. After Gina arrived with Chinese takeout last night, I told my friends I wanted to be alone. Alexander never texted me again, and I certainly didn't respond after he made it clear that there's nothing else to say. So, that means in two days I will return to Connecticut and make a fresh start—again. I wish I never sent that text. Actually, I take that back. I wish I had responded when Alexander was trying desperately to reach out to me.

Gina wanted to call Uncle Dominic for back up to take care of Alexander. Thankfully, Angie stopped her from making that call as she already had the phone in her hand. Angie's convinced that things will get work out when I get home. I'm not that optimistic.

Ugh. This is so pathetic. I need to pull myself together.

I drag myself out of bed, brush my teeth, and put some clothes on.

"Good morning," I say, joining my friends in the living room. I'm trying to sound as cheerful as I possibly can.

They're both wearing running clothes. Holy crap, did they already go running? What time is it?

"Good morning, we were just getting ready to grab some breakfast."

Hmm . . . I am pretty hungry. "That sounds good. I just want to take a quick walk on the beach," I say. I put a hat and sunglasses on to hide my bed head and my swollen eyes.

"That's a great idea. We'll come with you," Gina says, jumping off the couch.

I hold my hand up to stop her. "I just need a few minutes. I've decided I'm going to have one last good cry. Then, I'm coming back here and we're going to have an awesome day. I refuse to let another man ruin another vacation."

"Good for you," Angie yells. She's takes a long sip of her coffee.

"We'll grab breakfast when you get back."

I give her a grateful smile.

I walk down the path toward the sand. It's already hot outside, but there's a nice breeze off the ocean. I know I told

Angie and Gina that I would have one last cry, but for some reason there are no tears falling. Maybe I knew deep down that this was going to happen. As amazing as my time with Alexander was, I was always looking over my shoulder waiting for something to go wrong. There could be some deeper meaning here—like I was meant to meet Alexander to help me get over what happened with Jake. Or maybe we were meant to meet to help grow my business.

I stand at the water's edge with the waves crashing against my feet. I close my eyes and give myself a little pep talk once again. I know I'm going to be okay no matter what happens. For now, I'm going to enjoy the rest of this weekend with my wonderful friends and try not to worry about my life back home.

My stomach growls reminding me that it's time for breakfast. I begin to head back to our suite when something catches my eye . . . actually, someone.

I must be hallucinating because it looks like . . . Alexander, or maybe it's his long-lost twin. Either way, this gorgeous man is walking toward me.

Despite the rising temperatures, I'm completely frozen. When he approaches, my mouth drops open.

He looks exhausted, and he's dripping in sweat.

"Summer."

I open my mouth to speak but no words come out for a few seconds.

"What are you doing here? Your text . . ."

He hangs his head. "I didn't send that text."

I'm so confused.

"Melanie sent it. We were at a meeting, and she had access to my phone when your text came through."

I shake my head and start laughing. "Of course she did. I should've known."

He stands there still looking down at the stand.

"I fired her."

I stop laughing. What?

"Summer, I'm so sorry. I should have listened to you. I was so scared of how it would affect my work if I let her go that I almost lost you."

I wonder if this is what shock feels like. I woke up this morning ready to move on with my life without Alexander in it and here he is, right in front of me.

"I wanted to see you in person to tell you I was going to let her go. I've been in touch with some business associates in search of a new assistant. And then, Mrs. Rothera contacted me. She told me everything—what happened with Valerie and that you had left town. In the meantime, I caught Melanie with my phone and it all . . . well, let's say it wasn't pretty."

My head is spinning right now.

"Finding you here was even harder. Your friends are tough."

I give a half smile and nod my head. "It's supposed to be no boys allowed."

He gives a nervous laugh, and then reaches for my hand. I let him take it.

"Please tell me I'm not too late. I know I don't deserve you after everything, but I came all this way to tell you that I choose you. From the moment you walked into my office with the bare walls I knew . . . I fell in love with you that first day."

I know with all my heart that he's being completely honest with me. I can't believe the nightmare is finally over. Well, I guess I was right when I told my friends I would have another good cry, because slowly the tears start to fall down my cheeks. Last summer, my heart was broken at the beach. This summer, it's completely mended.

"You're not too late," I say softly.

Before I can say anything else, he engulfs me in his arms and lifts me up off the sand.

"I love you, Summer," he says between his overpowering kisses. "And I refuse to let anything or anyone else come between us ever again."

"I love you, too."

He places me gently down on the sand and takes my hand. As we walk along the beach, my hand in his, I place my head on his shoulder. My love of this season is restored, and after the wild year I've had, I'm overjoyed to feel like myself again and return to Summer.

Epilogue

*T*hankfully, Angie and Gina got over the whole "no boys allowed" rule for our beach weekend. They even invited Brett and Vinny to join us after Alexander crashed our party. I know Gina was beyond excited to break this rule. Her relationship is still way too new to be away from her man for that long. I completely understand how she feels, and since Melanie has been removed from the picture, it's like Alexander and I are starting over once again. It really is amazing what a difference a year can make.

The exciting news is that I'm finally moving out of my apartment this weekend, and I'm not moving in with Alexander. As tempting as it is to become the lady of my dream house, it didn't feel right just yet. Things are really good just the way they are.

Speaking of my move, Mrs. Rothera and I had a long talk when I returned from Florida. I've come to realize that her intentions are always good; she just needs to learn not to cross any boundaries. I made a promise to her that I would come visit her often and even let her give me advice from time to time.

I finally ordered the last of the furniture Helena requested for her apartment makeover, so I will soon be free of most of Alexander's past. And Helena just broke the news that she and Jacques are engaged. I couldn't be more thrilled for her and even more thrilled that Caroline (her best friend) was wrong about Helena and Alexander being soul mates.

Gina told me that she heard Jake was dating someone, and her name also happens to be Summer. What are the chances? Anyway, that seems kind of strange to me, but I wish him well.

Angie and Brett finally set a date for their wedding, and of course it's none other than Halloween of *next* year. We did make a life-long promise that we would spend every Halloween together for the rest of our lives—this year we're spending it at some big Halloween party at Disney World. I certainly don't mind. I still miss her a lot, and I get to take another trip to Florida.

Alexander hired a new assistant and he says she's doing a great job. She seems really nice, and best of all, she's happily married.

Summer Interiors is doing okay, unfortunately business has slowed down, but I'm hopeful that it will pick up again in the fall, just like this past year.

This year has been such a whirlwind, but looking back I wouldn't change a thing. Each season brings a new adventure, and I'm ready to move forward onto the next adventure, with Alexander right by my side.

THE END

Dear Reader

I hope you enjoyed *Return to Summer: A Novella*. Please take
a few minutes to leave a review on Amazon.

Love my books? Join my Facebook reader group.
Interested in a free book? Click here.

Visit my website for updates, and stay tuned for my next
book coming soon.

authormelissabaldwin.com

Poison in Paradise: a Tropical Romantic Mystery Now Available

Do you enjoy reading Cozy Mysteries?

Buy now or read with your Kindle Unlimited Membership!

Life on the open seas is everything Lexi Walker ever wanted! Her position as the part-time lifeguard and part-time Port Adventures coordinator for Epic Cruise Line has her traveling around the world and living her dream. And she has high hopes that her latest trip to the tropical Bahamas will be nothing short of magical.

Hopes that are dashed all too quickly.

What starts as a chance connection with a friend from her past, who is sailing on Epic to celebrate her recent marriage, turns into a deadly tragedy when Lexi finds the groom dead in a resort's hot tub! Was it an accident? Or something more sinister? Suddenly Lexi finds herself thrust into a potential murder investigation where everyone is hiding something and no one seems innocent. Between trying to help the widow in desperate need of support, sifting through the victim's friends and family who are anything but grieving, and trying to prove to her boss, the way-too-tempting Jack Carson, that she's an asset and not a liability to Epic Cruise Line, Lexi has her hands full.

"Melissa Baldwin's highly imaginative story is one filled with fun, excitement and romance."

—Readers Favorite Book Reviews

Also by Melissa Baldwin

COZY MYSTERY

Killer Couture: A Small-Town Cozy Mystery

Poison in Paradise: a tropical romantic mystery

Movie Scripts & Madness (The Madness and Murder Mysteries #1)

Room Service & Murder (The Madness and Murder Mysteries #2)

ROMANTIC COMEDY

Can't Hurry Christmas: A Holiday Romantic Comedy

Now That We Don't Talk: A Romantic Comedy

All the Christmas Vibes: A Holiday Romantic Comedy

Love in Overtime: A Sweet Small Town Hockey Romcom (Love on Thin Ice Multi-Author Series)

Soulmates and Slapshots: A Sweet Small Town Hockey Romcom (Love in Maple Falls Multi-Author Series)

Can We Talk?: A Romantic Comedy (Question #1)

I Think He Knows?: A Romantic Comedy (Question #2)

A Very Complicated Christmas: A Holiday Romantic Comedy

Unlucky Christmas: A Holiday Romantic Comedy

It Could Happen: A Romantic Comedy

Friends ForNever: A Romantic Comedy

One Way Ticket (written with Kate O'Keeffe)

Thanks for the Love: A Novella (Thankful #1)

Thanks for the Memories (Thankful #2)

Thanks for the Friendship (Thankful #3)

Love and Ohana Drama (Twist of Fate #1

Fate and Blind Dates (Twist of Fate #2)

Glances and Taking Chances (Twist of Fate #3)

On the Road to Love (Love in the City #1)

All You Need is Love (Love in the City #2)

From Runway to Love (Love in the City #3)

Fall Into Magic (Seasons of Summer #1)

Winter Can Wait (Seasons of Summer #2)

To Spring With Love (Seasons of Summer #3)

Return to Summer (Seasons of Summer #4)

See You Soon Broadway (Broadway #1)

See You Later Broadway (Broadway #2)

An Event to Remember (Event to Remember #1)

Wedding Haters (Event to Remember #2)

Not Quite Sheer Happiness (Event to Remember #3)

About the Author

USA Today bestselling author Melissa Baldwin always dreamed of sharing her stories with the world. She brought this vision to life, becoming an award-winning, bestselling author of over thirty romantic comedies and cozy mysteries. Melissa is also a wife, mother, new empty-nester, and travel advisor.

Her books feature charming, ambitious, and real women, whom she considers part of her tribe. Although she rarely takes a day off, when she's not writing, she enjoys quality time with her family, traveling, attempting yoga poses, and booking Disney vacations. Melissa still uses a paper planner, and her guilty pleasures include Beverly Hills 90210 reruns and General Hospital.